HEART OF THE MOUNTAIN

FRANKIE LOVE

C.M. SEABROOK

HEART OF THE MOUNTAIN

An angel.

It's the worst rainstorm in history when I find her
unconscious in the woods.

Sent from Heaven.

She's lost and alone, a newborn baby in her arms.

I will protect them.

My cabin is their shelter from the storm. Under my
care, no one can hurt them.

Whatever the cost.

But I'm not who she thinks I am.

And if she finds out, she'll keep on running.

My home is her home, my heart, her heart.

And I sure as hell don't want to break it.

Dear Reader,
Were you missing the mountains as much as we were?!

James is the virgin burly bearded baby daddy you've been waiting for.

Can you say that three times fast?

Try it.

A little louder now. Harder. Harder.

Yes. Yes.

Wait for it.

Ohhh, yessss.

Just.Like.That.

He likes it when you scream his name.

We like it when you come back for more. :)

Xo, Frankie & Chantel

CHAPTER ONE

James

Rain comes down in sheets around me, making it nearly impossible to see five feet in front of me. The river has swelled and the single bridge into town is impassible.

"Shit," I mutter, knowing it'll be a good week before the water recedes, and that's if the rain lets up.

At least I was smart enough to stock up on supplies the last time I headed down the mountain. And even if I do run low on canned and dried goods, I'm a more than capable hunter. I may not have grown up as a mountain man, but that's what I've become these past five years.

And while I sometimes miss having people to talk to, I know the alternative is worse than being alone.

I have my books to keep me company, and my old yellow lab, Banjo, who's currently barking at something hidden in the foliage. I whistle for him, knowing we need to get back to my cabin before the storm gets worse. Black, ominous clouds are rolling in, and thunder cracks in the distance. Rain continues to hammer down hard, making the path muddy and dangerous.

"Banjo, come here, boy," I call out.

The stubborn dog is whimpering now, nose stuck in the bushes.

"What do you have there?" I ask, walking toward him. I'm a few feet away when I realize that it's a woman under the foliage, her eyes closed, her face deathly pale. I rush toward her, pushing her auburn hair away from her forehead, which is ice cold. I press my fingertips to her neck, feeling for a pulse. For a second, I feel nothing, and I fear the worst, but then it's there, faint, but there.

A small whimper comes from her lips, and her eyes flutter slightly. "He-help."

"Okay," I say, trying to keep the alarm out of my voice. "I'm going to help you—"

A cry rings out, faint, but distinguishable. And when I lift her slightly in my arms, I see the baby that she cradles close to her chest.

Fuck. What kind of trouble is the girl in? And

why the hell is she out in the middle of the woods with a newborn? There's only one explanation - she's running from someone.

The last thing I need is trouble. It's what I've been hiding away from up in these mountains all these years. But I know I can't leave her. She'll die, and so will the baby.

They're both my responsibility now. At least until this rain lets up and I can drive them into town.

As carefully as I can, I lift the woman in my arms, doing my best not to hurt either her or the child. The infant bleats louder as I trek up the hill toward my cabin. It's a hungry cry. I've been around enough babies in my life to know that.

"This is not going to end well," I mumble as I use my foot to open the door to my cabin, grateful I left the fire burning, because the place is warm. Banjo follows me inside, looking at me like he knows trouble is brewing.

"It'll be fine," I say, more to myself than the dog as I lay the woman down on my bed.

I pull blankets around her, and she gives a small whimper when I take the baby from her arms. It's my first priority, knowing if it catches a fever, there's nothing I'll be able to do to save it. And with the bridge washed out, I'll never be able to get them to a hospital.

"I'm just going to get you both warm," I tell her, even though her eyes only open momentarily, before fluttering close again. I can't imagine what the girl has gone through, and I just hope I found them in time.

I work fast, unbundling the infant from its wet clothes, and wrapping it in warm blankets, rocking her until she settles. It's a little girl, her hair the same reddish hue as her mother's, and judging from the fact that she still has her umbilical cord, she's less than two weeks old.

"It's okay, little sparrow," I murmur, cradling her against my chest.

I have no idea what to do about food. I have no bottles, no milk. But thankfully the infant soothes, falling back to sleep, and I'm able to create a makeshift crib out of a dresser drawer and blankets.

When she's settled, I turn toward the woman lying in my bed. Her eyes are still closed, but she's trembling, and muttering incoherently in her sleep.

"Hey," I say, crouching beside her. "I need to get you out of your wet clothes."

Her lashes flutter open, and in the firelight, I catch a glimpse of browns, greens, and gold in her eyes, swirls of color that give me pause. She's beautiful, there's no denying that. But she's also in trouble. And she's going to be in even more trouble if I don't get her warm.

"I'm going to undress you, okay?"

She blinks, but then her eyes close again. As I start to peel the layers away, she barely responds. I try to be as gentle as I can with her, especially when I see the dark bruises on her arms.

"Fuck." Something stirs in my chest, a primal part of me that knows I have to protect her.

I loosen the buttons on her jeans, then peel them down over her hips. The woman is all curves that make my cock immediately stand at attention, but I try not to notice how fucking sexy the girl is, or how her breasts fill out the sheer bra she wears.

I try and avert my eyes as I lift her up and place her head and arms through one of my oversized sweatshirts, but I'm no saint, and by the time I'm finished, my balls are aching with a hunger that I've never experienced before.

It doesn't help that I've spent the last five years practically a hermit.

Sure, I've had offers when I've gone into town. But I'm not the kind of guy that messes around. And I'm also not the kind of guy who's exactly relationship material. Which means I'm a twenty-four-year-old virgin without many prospects.

I let out a heavy sigh as I take her wet clothes and hang them to dry.

She's got nothing on her, no form of identification, and she dozes back off before I can find out her story. I wrap a heavy wool quilt over her, knowing that right now what she needs more than anything is rest.

Her baby cries, and I pull her to my chest, not wanting to wake her mama. "Shhh, little sparrow," I whisper, looking out the cabin window at the turbulent rainstorm outside. "I got you now. It's okay."

I hold her close, praying she doesn't catch a cold, that she can recover from whatever hell her and her mama we're running from. It's a wild world out there, and nothing is sacred - not if you've seen what I've seen, or done what I've done.

But as the baby falls asleep in my arms, I know these two will be stronger for getting through whatever they've overcome. If they can survive the storm, they'll never fear the rain.

CHAPTER TWO

Marcie

Warmth surrounds me, and I snuggle deeper into it, not wanting to wake up. But there's something nagging at the back of my mind, a responsibility, or something I should be doing.

And then I hear a baby's cry, and I'm fully awake. I blink quickly,and sit up too fast, the world spinning as I try to focus.

"Lily," I cry out, memories flooding through my mind.

My sister Amy.

Her last words.

The pink, screaming, innocent bundle that was placed in my arms.

And then running.

Two days I ran. And stole. And hid.

It was a nightmare, thinking that at any

moment they would find me. Find Lily.

But the running wasn't the worst of it. It was my niece's cries, trying to prepare bottles from the formula I'd stolen over a pitiful campfire.

And then the rain started, and it wouldn't stop.

I got turned around in the woods, walked and walked until my feet were bleeding and exhaustion took over.

"She's right here," a deep, voice says from across the room.

Panic fills me, especially when I see the giant of a man walking toward me, holding Lily. There's something familiar about him. Something I can't place. Like I know him, even though I know we've never met.

"Where...where am I?" I glance around, my body still aching from sleeping outside on the hard ground, the cold rain and wind seeping into my bones until I couldn't walk anymore.

"You're safe. For now." He places Lily in my arms carefully, like he's been around babies all his life, even though he looks like he'd be more comfortable with an ax in his hand than a bottle. "I found you out in the woods and brought you back here."

"Where is here?"

"My cabin. We're twenty miles from Fox

Hollow." He runs a large palm over his beard and shakes his head. "How the hell did you get here?"

"I...I walked."

He frowns at me. "From town?"

I bite my lower lip, looking down at my niece. Tears fill my eyes at the painful memories, and I know I have to lie. If I want to give Lily a future - I have to. No one can know she's not mine. "Yeah, I was running...from my boyfriend."

The man continues to run a hand over his thick beard, studying me, something so familiar about those blue eyes. "He the one who hurt you?" he asks, fists clenching at his side. "Who bruised you black and blue?"

I swallow, then frown. "You saw my body?"

He looks away. "I had to get you changed, you were half unconscious and soaked through, and I needed to make sure this baby's mama would wake up."

A sharp pain stabs me. Lily's mama will never wake up. I press my lips against Lily's forehead, remembering the way Amy looked at me as she took her final breaths, the way she begged me to take care of her daughter.

"Thank you," I say, sitting up. "But I need to go. I need to—"

"You aren't going anywhere," he says, cutting me

off. "The only bridge out of the woods collapsed, and the storm is only getting worse. We're stuck here for at least a few days."

"I...I can't stay here," I say, hating the idea of staying with a man. My body curls in on itself, fear winding its way up my spine. The only men I've ever known were intent on hurting me ... and this man is bigger than all the rest. His arms are huge, the flannel shirt he wears is tight around his biceps and broad shoulders. And even though he doesn't look like he's going to hurt me, he's still a man.

"You don't have a choice." He sits on a chair opposite the bed and clasps his hands together. "Look, my name is James. I live out here, all alone. And I can see how that might be scary, but I won't hurt you. I want to protect you from whoever you're running from."

I look over at him, expecting to feel the familiar slice of fear cutting through me, but when our eyes meet, there is none of that. Instead, I see true concern in his eyes ... and something else too. It's not lust... it's different than that. Compassion?

Whatever it is, it's not something I've ever seen in the hell that I just escaped from.

Blinking my emotions away, I refuse to consider that. No man has ever tried to keep me safe, protected, or sheltered from the brutality of the world. Why should James be any different? But right now I have no choice but to try and trust him.

"Want to tell me your name?" he asks, patience in his words. Another thing I'm not used to.

"I'm Marcie," I tell him, knowing I have to stay here until the storm dies down. "And this is Lily. She's a week old."

Lily starts fussing in my arms again and worry flares up inside of me. I have never looked after a child before and have no idea what to do.

"She's hungry," he says, looking at my chest. "And uh, not to be clinical here - but I'm figuring your milk never came in?"

"What?" My eyes widen as I take in this hulk of a man talking about my boobs.

"You weren't leaking, and it's been a few hours since I carried you here."

I shake my head, confused. "I..."

"She needs milk and you don't have any," he says blatantly.

Finally, I understand what he's getting at. "My backpack," I say, looking around. "Where is it?"

"You didn't have anything with you when I found you," he tells me.

I close my eyes. Shit. "I dropped it before I slipped. It has several cases of formula."

James is already standing, grabbing a big coat

from a hook. "You stay here. I'll go after it. Lily needs a bottle, getting her fed is all that matters right now."

I nod, trembling as he grabs a rifle. "Thank you."

"Banjo will watch over you until I get back," he says, nodding at the golden lab who lifts his head and looks at me from his bed by the fire. Then James heads out the cabin door without another word.

Alone in a stranger's cabin, I look around the simple room, wondering if running from the Wild Ride Motorcycle gang was the right decision. A question I've been pondering about for the last three days, ever since I escaped from my captors.

Except they weren't really my captors. I chose to live with them, following my sister in hopes of a better life.

But it wasn't better. I left one hell for another ... and now I have nothing. Lily wails in my arms and I rock the little one. She needs me to be strong, but tears streak my face as I think about all we've lost.

Waiting for James to return, I pray to a god I've never believed in. I pray that today the storm will pass and the sun will break through. Because I've had one too many dark days. I'm ready for some light.

CHAPTER THREE

James

Lily takes a bottle like a champ, and I spend the next couple of days rocking her, feeding her, changing her, and cradling her in my arms, as her mother sleeps. Marcie is resting as if she's been running for her life for a long ass time. Like this is the first time in her life that she's ever felt safe enough to rest. She's woken up a few times, barely eating, opening up a little bit before falling back into a heavy slumber.

And when Marcie sleeps, she looks so angelic with her curly auburn hair tousled around her face, her soft creamy skin so pure. She has curves that would tempt any man, but I try to keep my focus on Lily - not the gorgeous redhead in my bed. But it's nearly impossible.

In the short conversations I've had when she's

been awake, what I have learned about her is she's smart, with a quick sense of humor, and despite everything she's gone through, there's an innocence to her, a quiet strength.

I've caught her watching me when she doesn't think I'm aware. And I've seen the blush that creeps across her cheeks when her eyes fall to my chest. The way her pupils grow big and dark whenever I've brushed the back of my hand across her forehead, checking for a fever.

God, the woman already has me in knots. I want to protect, keep her safe, but there's also something primal inside of me that wants more...that wants to possess her, to make her mine.

I shake my head at the thought, knowing the longer she stays here, the more trouble I'm in. But I can't help but let my thoughts drift to the possibility of her and Lily staying with me for good.

I'm sitting in the rocking chair in front of the fire when Marcie stirs, stretching, she groans.

"God, I smell so gross," she says, cringing. "I need a shower so freaking bad." My lip turns to a smile and she catches me. "God, I do, don't I? Am I totally grossing you out?"

"Hardly," I tell her, my cock twitching as she puts her feet down on my hardwood floor. Marcie is beautiful, petite and curvy and so damn cute she makes me want to scoop her up in my arms. Nothing about her is remotely undesirable. Truth is, it's been a struggle to get any rest the last few nights because all I can think about is her creamy skin, my cock inside of her - taking care of her the way she so desperately needs.

She needs a man who will protect her, not hurt her.

I could be that man.

Not that I know anything much about her. But damn, I want to.

"Lily is fast asleep. Go help yourself to a shower," I tell her, placing the infant in the small crib. "I'll get you a change of clothes and make you something to eat."

Marcie gives me a grateful smile before kneeling down and kissing Lily's forehead.

She heads to the bathroom to take her shower and I set a change of clothes just inside the door.

"James?" she asks, her silhouette clear through the sheer curtain.

"Just leaving some clothes," I say, my voice rough. The steam of the shower curling around me, making it hard to think clearly.

When I look at her, it isn't just about a hungry cock - it's about this primal urge to wrap my arms around her and never let a soul hurt her, ever again.

She pokes her head around the curtain, her face brightened considerably in just those few minutes. The hot water must be just what she needs. And I'm not surprised, considering she gave birth such a short time ago ... no wonder she's been sleeping so hard - she is still recovering.

"Thanks," she says. "God, this feels so incredible."

"Good," I say. I've always been a man of few words, and this is no exception. If I say much more right now, I'll scare Marcie away like a skittering little rabbit.

"Do you have any shampoo?" Her voice is as sweet as honey. "You've only got a bar of soap in here."

I frown. "Sorry, wasn't expecting company."

"It's okay," she says. "This is better than nothing." She squeezes her eyes shut. "Sorry, that sounded rude."

"Not rude," I say. "Just honest." My hand is on the doorknob and I'm aiming to leave just as soon as she stops talking. "I'm gonna go then, I want to respect your privacy... I mean it's only a curtain keeping me from feasting on you." I regret the words the second I say them. *Nice job at keeping your cool, man*, my head reprimands.

But Marcie doesn't yell at me to get out like I

expect her to, she just lifts her brows, and her pink tongue swipes over her lips.

"Shit, sorry, I didn't mean..." I rub my palm over the back of my neck. "I'll go make us some dinner."

"Thanks," she says, her voice almost a whisper, and I swear when she says, "I'm hungry too," she's not talking about food.

"I'm fucking starved," I growl out, turning before I say anything else I might regret.

But I swear to God she whimpers behind me. It takes all my restraint not to claim her then and there. But she's a little bird with a wounded wing and my goal right now is to help her take flight, not tie her down with my own needs.

I leave the bathroom and close the door, resting my back against the wall in the hallway, my cock a fucking force to be reckoned with. If it was just me here, all alone in this cabin, I'd take care of my hard-on, but it's a one-room cabin - perfect for me ... but sweet Lily is all alone out there. I'm not gonna climb the ladder to the loft just to jack off.

So I step out on the covered front porch for a moment, the frosty air helping me with my aching cock. When I've cooled off, I head back inside, and find Marcie pulling open a cupboard door on her tiptoes in one of my t-shirts, it hits her at her thigh, and she opted not to pull on my sweats that would be about ten sizes too big.

Fine with me.

Though my cock might not appreciate seeing so much skin. God, she looks incredible.

"Hey," she says. "I thought I could help with dinner."

Running a hand over my beard, I shake my head. "No, you shouldn't be on your feet."

"Let me do this," she says. "I have to repay you somehow."

Frowning, I step toward her. "Repay me for what?"

"You saved my life. Lily's life. We wouldn't have survived out there if you hadn't have found us."

I wave it off, not wanting to be thanked for doing my duty - giving a woman and her child shelter from the worst storm this region has seen in a hundred years - any man would do that. But even as I think it, I know the truth. I grew up surrounded by men who believed women were property to do with as they pleased, and to be discarded whenever they weren't of use anymore.

I've spent my adult life running from men like that and vowing never to be one of them.

"James," Marcie says, reaching for my hand. "I mean it. Thank you. And thank you for taking care of Lily. I was clearly exhausted. How long did I sleep?"

"Two days," I tell her, pulling out some cans of soup and grabbing a pot.

"I'd been running for three days before you found us," she says softly, her body so close to mine, and it takes all my self-control not to wrap my arms around her. "I hadn't slept at all. And then the rain started."

I turn on the stove and begin stirring the lentil soup. "Well, the storm is still raging. The radio says it's predicted to last through the week. Once it passes, we can get you where you need to go."

"Right," she says, wrapping her arms around herself. "I'll go as soon as possible. I'm sure you're more than ready for us to be out of your hair."

I lift an eyebrow, reaching for bowls and spoons, and grinning down at her. "Hardly. I've been alone a long ass time, it's not the worst thing to have some company."

Reaching for a beer in the fridge, I offer her one. She accepts it and we clink the necks of the bottles.

"Cheers," she says, her eyes not meeting mine.

"To life," I say, thinking how grateful I am that I was out on my property when she was in desperate need of help.

But she doesn't take my words well, instead, her eyes glass over and she repeats my toast with tears filling those gorgeous hazel eyes.

"Shit, what is it?" I ask, setting down my beer and stepping closer.

"Nothing," she says. "Just ... I lost my sister recently. She died and ... and it's hard to imagine the world without her. Without her life."

"Fuck," I say, resting a hand on her shoulder. "You really have been through hell, haven't you?"

She looks up at me, her bottom lip trembling. "That's only the half of it."

"I don't doubt that." I swallow, wishing I could pull her in my arms, wipe her tears away, but what she really needs is a nourishing meal, not a stranger to make a pass at her. "Soup is probably ready. Are you hungry?" The words we exchanged in the bathroom floating through my brain as I say them again.

She gives a forced smile and nods. "Yeah."

I clear my throat and ladle the soup into bowls, then sit with her at the table made for two. Lily sleeps only a few feet away from us and I look over to check on her, smiling when I see the sweet cherub face.

"You're so good with her." Marcie picks up her spoon and my shoulders relax when she takes a few bites. Seeing her eat is a good sign. She needs to regain her strength.

"I had lots of practice growing up," I tell her. "Lots of cousins."

"Do you see them much?" she asks.

"No. Not as much as I'd like." Truth is, I ran just like her. But unlike her, it was because I was too much of a coward to bring assholes like the boyfriend she's running from to justice. "I don't go into town very often, not since..." I sigh and open up more than I have to anyone in a long time. "Not since my mom died."

"I'm sorry," she says, resting her hand on mine for a moment. And I feel like she understands me. I don't know her story and she doesn't know mine, but I have a feeling we both understand loss in a way lots of other people don't.

"Well, I'm grateful for the practice you had," she says, pulling her hand away. "Lily is reaping the benefits right now." She stands up and goes to the counter to grab us napkins.

"It's no problem. She's an angel. Just like her mom," I say, scooting back from the table, taking a long pull from my beer.

Marcie turns toward me, napkins in hand. Her eyes meet mine then, and I swear for a moment I think I've said the wrong thing. But then she steps toward me and cups my cheek with her hand. "You're a good man, James."

Despite the warning in my head that I'm over-stepping, I pull her toward me, my hand on her hips and she steps closer, between my legs. She's small and fits perfectly. Our eyes lock and I can feel the need inside me grow, it's thick and hot.

God, she's so damn close.

Close enough to kiss...close enough for so much more.

I know she feels it too, because she dips her head to mine, brushing her lips softly across my own. But then Banjo begins to bark, and she pulls back quickly.

The kiss was chaste, a thank you, a moment in time that I wish would last the whole night through.

"Marcie," I start, but she shakes her head, step-ping back.

"Sorry, " she says. "I shouldn't have."

"I'm glad you did." I sigh, dragging my fingers through my hair.

Whoever Lily's father might be - he's a fucking bastard to hurt the two girls in my cabin now. Though Marcie is certainly no girl - with curves like hers, she is all woman.

That cock of mine twitches again and I groan,

needing it to keep itself out of sight. Marcie is in a lot of pain right now and doesn't need to think I'm only thinking about fucking her.

Because in truth, I'm not thinking that. I'm thinking about caressing her, stroking her, kissing her until she melts, until the tension in her shoulders fades and her body is a puddle of pleasure - no more pain.

Marcie hands me a napkin, but before my fingertips touch it, it falls to the floor. She bends over, and I see she isn't wearing her panties. Bare-bottomed and so fucking cute that the curve of her ass sends my mind into a fucking tailspin - but then I see it. The tattoo on her lower back.

Except it's not a tattoo. It's a brand. A mark burned into her soft flesh.

Anger sizzles inside of me, growing into an inferno, because I know who did that to her. And in a flash, I understand who she is running from. Why she'd be so damn desperate to leave.

She's been branded by the leader of the Wild Ride MC.

My father.

CHAPTER FOUR

Marcie

"The rain is still coming down hard," I say when James comes out on the covered porch with me.

I've been here almost a week, and there doesn't seem to be any end in sight to the flooding. Not that I mind. I don't want to leave. And it's not just because I have no idea where Lily and I are going to go.

I don't want to leave James.

I've known a lot of men in my life. Bad men. My father was a mean drunk who had no trouble putting his hands on me and my sister whenever he was angry. I think that's why she ran off with the first man who made eyes at her. And of course I followed her, right into a pit of vipers.

I was sixteen when the Wild Ride MC took us in. At first it wasn't all bad. I was left alone to my books most of the time. And in the evenings I helped at the bar. Sometimes men got too handsy, but I learned how to deal with them.

And then Amy got pregnant.

I know the abuse started before then, but slowly she became a skeleton of the strong girl I'd known. I'd begged her to run away with me, but she said they'd kill her. And in a way they had.

I shiver now, memories assaulting me. James' arms wrap around me, and he pulls me against his side and rubs my arms. It's a simple gesture, intimate, and full of heat that we've both been trying to ignore the past week.

"You should go in. It's cold out here." His voice is gruff, and when I glance up at him, I see him scanning the woods, like he's looking for danger.

He's been more broody, more withdrawn the past few days than he had been when I first arrived, and I worry that he's getting annoyed with us being here.

But then he looks down at me, and my insides melt, and a sense of belonging warms me from the inside out. I've had men look at me with lust before, but the way James looks at me is different.

I see the desire, the hunger and need, but there's also tenderness. My core aches, my skin tingles with anticipation. I kissed him once, but

I'd pulled back, worried that I'd mistaken his signals.

But there's no mistaking the way he's looking at me now.

"James." His name on my lips sounds more like a whimper. I want him to kiss me. The thought of his mouth on mine, his large calloused hands roaming my body, it consumes my dreams.

After what happened with my sister, I never thought I'd feel this way about a man.

But I trust James - completely.

"Marcie," he says, voice gruff, palms cupping my jaw, mouth so close to mine I can feel his warm breath on my lips. "You have to stop looking at me that way, sweetheart."

"Why?"

His thumb traces my bottom lip.

"Because you have no idea what I want to do to you. And you..." He sighs and rests his forehead against my own. "You just had a baby."

Tell him the truth, my brain screams.

And I'm about to when a crash sounds in the distance.

James jumps back on full alert. And my own heart begins to thump like it's outside my chest.

They found me. It's my first thought. And I know my next actions are irrational, but fear seizes me.

I run into the cabin and grab Lily, ready to run. I don't even bother looking for my shoes. I need to get out of here, now. It's James who stops me from bolting out the door.

"Slow down." He takes my shoulders, holding me firmly and forcing me to look at him. "You're okay. It was just a tree falling."

"A...a tree." My breathing is labored. "You're sure?"

He nods, gently taking Lily from my arms and placing her back in her makeshift crib.

I'm trembling when he turns back to me and pulls me into his arms. "You're safe."

I shake my head against his chest. "I'll never be safe."

He sighs, tilting my chin up. "I'll do whatever I can to make sure you and Lily are. I promise you that, Marcie. Even if you don't want to tell me what happened."

"I want to tell you." My hands fist in his shirt, and I know it's time. "Do you have anything stronger than beer?"

His lips twist up and he nods. "I have a bottle of Glengoyne I've been saving." He moves toward one of the cupboards, crouching and pulling out a bottle.

"This stuff is expensive," I say, taking the bottle

from him when he hands it to me.

"You know your whisky?" he asks one brow raised when he sets two glasses on the table.

I shrug. "I tended bar at the Wild Ride Club for the past two years, so I got to know a few things."

James tenses. I see it, and I know why, he's realizing just how much trouble I'm actually in. But he doesn't ask questions, just pours two large shots, then hands me one.

I take a sip, then shoot the whole shot back, needing the liquid courage to tell him the truth, of facing the memories.

He pours me another shot when I sit down at the table, pulling my knees to my chest, and tell him how Amy and I ended up being part of one of the most notorious motorcycle gangs in the state of Wyoming.

I tell him everything.

"Lily's your niece?" There's no judgment in his eyes, but I can see him processing everything.

I nod, sipping at the aged whisky. "I had to leave. Amy begged me to take her. And I knew..." I glance away from those intense blue eyes that study me now. "You don't know what they'd have done to me." I shiver in fear at what I'd overheard. "I heard them talking about selling my virginity—"

James pushes his chair back and stands so fast it

topples to the floor. He curses loudly, but thankfully Lily only stirs in her sleep and doesn't wake up.

"I'm sorry for bringing you into this," I say, chewing on my bottom lip.

"You don't have to be sorry about anything." His words are intense, and when he crouches in front of me, there's a violence in his eyes. Not directed at me, but I know he wants vengeance. And it scares me, because I don't want him to get hurt.

"I'm sorry for lying to you."

"I understand why you did." He takes my hands and brings them to his lips. "Thank you for trusting me enough to tell me."

"I'm not sure what I'm going to do." I wipe the tears away, wanting to be strong, but James' eyes tell me he will be my strength right now.

"You'll stay here. You and Lily. I'll keep you safe. I already promised you that. This changes nothing. Except..." He glances away, his jaw clenching like he's holding something back.

I touch his cheek, run my fingers over his beard. He's so handsome. "Except what?"

He looks back at me, and what I see is a starving man. "You were honest with me, so I'll be honest with you. I want you, Marcie. So fucking bad my balls ache with it. But I won't push you—"

I bury my hands in his hair and kiss him, hard. He groans against my mouth, and picks me up, wrapping my legs around his waist. And I tell him what I've been craving to tell him for the past week, "I want you, too."

CHAPTER FIVE

James

Her lips are soft, just like I imagined. She holds on to me, as if for dear life, and maybe right now - that is what this is. Life or death. Marcie's body presses against mine with a need that is desperate and raw. A need I understand. Because my body thrums to life with desire for her, to be her one and only. *Her everything.*

"God, Marcie," I groan, my hands running down her back, drawing her closer. I've saved myself for this moment - for her.

We roll into my bed, and with the baby asleep, we begin to undress one another, slowly, and with intention, knowing this moment is electric and ours. So much of our lives haven't been our own. But this? This is ours and we aren't sharing any of it.

I lift the hem of her t-shirt, slipping it over her head. Her round, full tits are beautiful, like every inch of her skin. She's naked in my bed, her ass so creamy, her pussy untouched and tight.

Marcie unbuttons my flannel shirt, her warm hands running over my bare chest, my ladder of abs tightening as she touches them.

I kick off my jeans, my boxers, and the two of us are naked, our souls bared to one another as we gently explore each other's bodies. Facing one another, I run my hands over her, massaging her tits and drawing her close for a kiss. My cock is hard and being pressed against her belly makes me solid steel.

She gingerly touches me, her hand on my cock, and I run my fingers between her thighs, her pussy hot with want. I groan, wanting her so fucking bad.

"I don't want to do this wrong," she says, her voice a whisper.

"You won't, I promise, little bird."

"But I've never done this and—"

I cut her off. "I never have either."

Her eyes widen. "Never?"

I shake my head. "Not once. I'm a virgin too, Marcie. I saved myself for you."

She licks her lips. "You didn't even know me, James."

"I saved myself for the woman who would make me feel like a man, who'd make me feel like I do with you. Like I could take down armies in your name, like I could march into battle for your honor. A woman I'd lay down my life for."

Tears fill her eyes. "James..."

"Don't cry," I tell her, cupping her beautiful face in my palm. "But believe me, Marcie. When I make love to you, it's no small thing. It is everything."

She wraps her arms around me, and I roll on top of her, my girl - my world.

"You make me feel like I'm more than my past. When you look at me, James, it's like ... like you see our future."

"I do Marcie. I see a whole fucking world just waiting for us."

She clings to me and I kiss her again, softly. My lips are promises I intend to keep. She's been through hell, but this moment, right now it's heaven.

I move down the bed, spreading her knees and running my tongue over her, her pussy sweet and wet and all mine. My cock groans in pleasure, this moment, right here, is one I've been waiting my entire life for. There are things about me she doesn't know - but I will tell her everything in good time.

Right now, this night, is about the present - not the past. So I lick her tight pussy, her hips wiggling, her back arching, the gentle moans of pleasure escaping her heart-shaped mouth. I know she loves it, and so do I. She drips for me and I press a finger inside of her, wanting to explore every inch of her perfect body. She's so tight and my cock is so damn big, but I know if I kiss her enough, get her ready, she will be able to take me.

Fingering her is a fucking fantasy. I've never touched a woman before - never run my hands over a woman's thighs and planted kisses on her folds. And God I'm glad I've waited for the one.

My one.

It's been a week of falling for her and damn, I know she's been through so much and isn't ready for my declarations - so instead I will show her my devotion by worshipping her body.

"Oh, James," she whimpers as I lick her slit up and down, her pussy clenching as I inhale her. "Please, let me touch you," she begs. "Please."

I flick my tongue over her, teasing her as her toes curl, her legs wrapping around my shoulders, and I smile as I breathe her in. As she nears the edge of her pleasure, I wrap my hands around her hips and squeezing her ass as I dip my tongue deeper inside her heat.

"Don't make me wait," she moans. "Oh...oh."

The swirl of my tongue against her warmth causes her moaning to grow louder. My beard tickles her as she gets off against me in the way I've been dreaming about since the moment I first laid eyes on her curvy body.

She finishes, panting with happiness and I move on top of her once more. "God, I love your pretty little cunt," I tell her, kissing her hard.

She smiles, the wall between us gone, it fell away the moment we gave in to our desire. And now there's nothing left to do except make love all night.

"Come here," she tells me, a teasing smile tugging at her lips. "Let me find out what all the fuss is about."

She runs her hands over my length, her eyes widening as she takes hold of my girth. I'm a fucking stallion and this pretty little virgin is going to ride me.

"You think you can handle it?"

She smiles. "You should realize I can get through anything."

Those words are so damn true, and hell, they make me want her all the more. "Then come here, sweet one, let's go somewhere we've never been before."

CHAPTER SIX

Marcie

When James begins to fill me, inch by perfect inch, it takes all my strength to not weep. Not because it hurts - but because it feels so damn good. Being here, in his protective embrace, his body my shelter from the storm outside this cabin, fills me with a sense of security I've never felt before.

He smells so good, like a wood fire and cedar trees and the air after it's rained. Fresh and clean and mine. I breathe him in, his body the oxygen I've been craving all my life. I can't get enough, and I press my palms against his chest, refusing to forget a second of our time together.

"Oh God," he growls in my ear. "You're so fucking tight, my cock needs you, girl."

And I whimper beneath him, wanting to give his hungry cock the meal it needs.

"Don't stop," I plead as he moves against me, our rhythm written in the sky. The rain brought us together and the storms of life melded our hearts as one.

"Never."

I know it's crazy to think of a future with a man I've just met ... but life is crazy.

And hard.

And lonely.

So very lonely.

But when I'm with James, in his cabin, sweeping the floorboards or washing dishes, I feel like I am finding a real footing for the first time in my life. I feel like I belong here, with him. A man as honest and as forthright as I've ever met.

When he looks at me, I believe he has told me the whole story, and that makes me feel like his cabin in the woods is a cocoon, the netting I needed. Not a trap, instead, it's a blanket keeping me warm.

His body is a river of muscles, and I want to swim in him. He thrusts his thickness inside me, and I moan, the strength of him intoxicating, and I want to bathe in it, drown in him, and never leave this feeling of weightlessness.

"Marcie," he groans, cupping my cheek as he takes me to the very brink of pleasure. To the very edge of the world. "I'm gonna come, sweetheart."

I arch my back as he thrusts deeper inside me, giving myself over to him in every sense of the word. We are virgins no longer, we are making sweet love in the middle of nowhere, our hearts bound, pounding as we meet in the middle, both of us coming undone and stitching ourselves back together all at once.

My body tenses as I reach a pinnacle of desire that I've never imagined possible. My body lets go and I release everything I've kept bottled up inside. Every inch of my skin is on fire, fueled by desire and as James kisses me, it only fans the flame.

He wraps his arms around me so tight, I can hardly breathe. He is hanging on for dear life, same as me. I won't let go.

Our eyes meet and we breathe as one, our hearts beating in sync, our bodies still joined.

"I love you, Marcie," he tells me.

I kiss him, words not adequate for the swell of emotions wrapping around my bruised and beaten heart.

———

The next morning a weight has been lifted in the

cabin. The rain still drops on the metal roof, but the sun is breaking through the clouds and a stream of light filters through the window. Banjo is at the foot of the bed, and Lily is nestled between James and me, her tiny body swaddled in a pale pink blanket that someone gave her at Wild Ride. Not sure who and I wish I knew. Because it is one of her only possessions.

"What are you thinking?" James asks, tucking a strand of my curly hair behind my ear.

"Lily will never know her mom. It breaks my heart."

"What happened to her?" he asks softly.

After making love several times last night, we showered. A barrier dropped after we lost our virginity and smiles covered our faces as we stole glances at one another, washing up with soap and warm water, our hands exploring every inch the other had to offer. We dressed in clean t-shirts and underwear, then gave Lily a new bottle and a diaper change. We fell asleep with this angel between us.

"The guy who was in charge of her - the leader of the pack. A man named Clay, he basically owned her."

James sucks in a deep breath and I wonder what he is thinking right now. Probably that he wishes he knew Clay so he could beat him to the ground.

James would do that - anything in his power to protect me from a man like that.

"Anyway, Amy was his property and he didn't want anyone to touch her. Not even doctors. He had one of the women at the club come in when she went into labor, this girl had gone to nursing school for awhile before dropping out, so she knew more than the rest of us about childbirth ... but she still didn't know enough."

I get choked up thinking about Amy, how vulnerable she was. How all the men at Wild Ride had the women under their thumb. We couldn't go anywhere, couldn't run, couldn't get help - we were under their control. Guns have a way of keeping even the strongest person down. And those men had plenty.

"After Lily came into the world, it was clear Amy was losing too much blood. She was weak and pale, hemorrhaging. We begged Clay to call 911, but he refused. He was scared, I saw it in his eyes. He knew Amy wasn't going to make it and he decided losing her was better than losing the entire community he built. If the police stepped one foot on his compound, he'd be locked up for good."

"And if anyone spoke out against him, they would be dead and buried, too."

I nod. "Exactly. Clay was the boss. *Is* the boss."

My breathing shallows as I consider what he will do to me if he finds me. "I never want to go back there."

"You won't," he tells me. His words last night flood my heart, *I love you*, and they make me brave, help me tell the rest of this painful story.

"Amy died the next morning, we couldn't get the bleeding to stop and I don't think any of the other men even knew what was happening. They were drunk or high and it was just Mickey and me. She was our friend and after Amy passed away, she was the one and only reason I got Lily out of there. She saved us. And I don't want to imagine the price she paid for it."

"No other women were there to help you?"

I shake my head. "No. Clay started another compound in Idaho last year and sent the other women there. I have no idea where it even is."

"God, Marcie, you went through so much." His eyes pierce mine.

"I've decided that when the storm stops, I'm going to the police, and telling them everything. Clay is a murderer. I just don't understand why other people who knew this about him, the people who left, wouldn't have gone to the cops."

"It sounds like he's gone from bad to worse -

with this new compound, what he did to your sister. Maybe he wasn't always like that."

I kiss Lily's forehead. "I think you're right. I heard he used to be a lot less cruel. Back when his wife and son were alive. But after they died, it's like he snapped."

"I'm so sorry Amy's gone," James says, our fingers lacing together.

Tears fall down my cheeks, her death so raw, so recent. It's going to take a long time for my heart to heal.

"I shouldn't have told you I loved you last night, you need space, time to heal—"

I cut James off. His words are kind, but he's wrong. "No. I don't. Your words are the balm I need."

Our hands squeeze tight, tears filling both our eyes. I've never known this before - love. I'm still scared to say it back, but that's okay for now. James is more than the man who took my virginity - he is the man who stole my heart.

CHAPTER SEVEN

James

Days have passed and finally the storm has let up. Marcie and Lily are fast asleep when I walk outside with Banjo, the morning sun just rising behind the mountain. I breathe in the fresh, dewy air, standing on the porch. The rain has stopped, which means the river will start to recede soon, and the bridge will be passable again. Which is good, because we're running low on resources.

But it also scares the shit out of me, because I know my father, and he won't sit back and let one of his brands run away so easily, especially not when she took something that he believes belongs to him - Lily. *My half-sister.*

I have no doubt he has men already scouring this mountain.

The truth, which I haven't told her, is that she

won't ever be safe. Not as long as my old man is alive.

I know, because he came close to killing me - his own son. All because I refused to become one of them. He told his club that I died, just like my mother did all those years ago. And in his mind, I did. Leaving meant that in his eyes, I'm a traitor.

And I'm a liar. At least to Marcie.

I haven't told her who I am. I know I have to. But I don't want her to think of me like that. I may have run from that life, but before I did I committed crimes I'm not proud of. I hate the boy I was. Which is why I've fought all these years to become the man I am now.

I sit down on the porch and stare down at the yellowed photo in my hand. It's the only one I kept. The only picture I have of my mom. She was pretty, with long dark hair that hung down to her waist, but even then, her eyes were hollow, empty, like the bastard she'd called her old man had already beaten the life out of her.

I'm only about twelve in the photo, and I hate the way I look up at my father, like he's some kind of superhero and not the supervillain I know him to be now.

The door creaks open behind me, and I shove the photo in my pocket.

"It stopped raining." A blanket wrapped around her shoulders, her hair tousled, cheeks glowing, Marcie sits down beside me and rubs Banjo's head.

I pull her into my lap and kiss her.

"It's a good omen, right?" Marcie's eyes flicker with light and she leans against me, her body warm.

"You ready for your present?"

She shakes her head in confusion. "Present?"

"You didn't really think I was chopping wood in the rain, did you?"

She laughs. "I thought you just needed some space."

"Just a sec." I leave her on the porch and head to my woodshop just a few yards from the cabin. I lift the piece I made from the ground and carry it back to the front porch.

"What in the world...." Marcie's eyes water and she brushes away her tears as she takes in my craftsmanship.

Pieces of cedar sanded and stained, a cradle nailed together for Lily.

Her niece and my half-sister.

I want to tell Marcie everything - about my father, my past, my story, but I don't want to hurt her. Not when she is only now finding her strength.

Still, I have to be honest - I need to tell her everything.

She wraps her arms around me before I can say the words that will push her away. "Oh, James, it's so perfect. Let's put her in it now," she says already stepping into the cabin.

Marcie lifts Lily from her makeshift crib, smiling as wide as I've ever seen her. I place the handmade cradle at the foot of our bed and watch as Marcie sets the still sleeping Lily in her newly crafted cradle. "It's the sweetest thing, James," she gushes, her happiness my only goal. The last thing I want to do right now, when she's wearing a smile like this, is erase it with a story that will only confuse her healing heart.

"Come here," she says, taking my hand. "Sit down."

I lift a brow, wondering what it is she wants. I sit down on the bed, and take her hand, knowing I can't put this off any longer. "I need to talk to you, Marcie. It's important."

She licks her lips. "Please, let me do this first."

"Do what?"

She drops to her knees and begins tugging off the belt on my blue jeans, pulling down the zipper, her eyes widening with excitement.

"Baby, we need to talk," I try again.

She shakes her head. "Please, let me try this. I want to thank you, James. And I have a feeling you'll like this."

I run my hands through her hair, then lift her chin. "What I have to say will change things between us, Marcie."

She steels her eyes. "Then don't say a word. If everything is bound to change, then let me have this. Please."

I stop fighting it, wanting to give Marcie everything she wants. She pulls my cock from my jeans and opens her mouth, taking me between her lips, and I close my eyes, letting this angel take care of me the way I need. God, she feels so good, her pink lips wrapped around my cock and I'm so fucking hard, my guilt laces with pleasure and I groan, pressing her head down, so she can take me deeper. She whimpers, enjoying my dominance, the way I am guiding her. She purrs, deep throating me, her fingers on my aching balls, her fingers running up and down my shaft as she sucks me, hard.

"Fuck," I growl, so damn close.

"Come," she pants. "Let me taste you," she begs. It doesn't take much - her horny words force my cock to erupt. She sucks harder, swallowing every drop of my milky cum, and she loves it, swirling her tongue over my tip, holding my balls in her hand and squeezing them ever so gently.

"That okay?" she asks, blinking sweetly.

"You're a fucking treasure, Marcie."

She looks up at me with such trusting eyes I have to look away. I need to tell her everything. But Lily starts fussing and Marcie stands. "I think she needs a bottle."

In the kitchen, she opens and closes cupboards as I pull up my pants.

"Shit," she whispers, holding up an empty can of formula. "We're all out. When I fed her in the middle of the night, I didn't realize she finished it."

"I think there might be one more," I say, looking in the pantry. "A-ha!" I hand her the can. "But I should go to town. We'll need more by the end of the day and besides, with the flooding receding, I think I can get my truck down the mountain."

"Thank God," Marcie says, relief in her voice. She begins making a bottle as Lily stirs in her new cradle. "Can you get some diapers, too? Because I'm pretty much over this whole cloth situation."

I kiss Marcie on the lips. "Of course. Let's make a list."

A few minutes later we've put together a list of

what I need to get us in town. I grab my jacket and lace up my boots.

"Did you need to talk about something?" she asks. She's got Lily in her arms, feeding her a bottle.

The last thing I want to do is leave the house in a fight - and if I open this cluster-fuck of worms, I know it's gonna take awhile to recover. "When I come back."

"It's not too awful, is it?"

I smile at her, kissing her and Lily on the forehead. "We can get through anything."

The sky above may be clear, but as I walk away, Marcie's eyes cloud over. This, right here, what we just had the last few weeks, might be as good as it ever gets.

CHAPTER EIGHT
Marcie

"Look, little sparrow," I say, using the nickname James gave Lily. I'm sitting on the porch and rocking her as I smile up at rainbow that stretches across the sky. "I think it's a sign."

Hope.

That's what I feel. What I'm choosing to hold onto, even if James' words were ominous. And I can't help the goofy grin that stretches across my face as I think about James. Of the life we can have. All the promises he's made. And I let my guard down -- completely, and just let hope wrap around me.

James headed into town after my *thank you* for the cradle to pick up much-needed supplies. But we have almost everything we need up here. Far away from danger.

"We're going to be alright," I whisper, believing it's true. I know James said he needed to talk - but I have a feeling he has a sad past just like me. I want to believe that whatever it is, we can get through it. Together.

But I should have learned a long time ago, that hope is only an illusion. There's always darkness lurking around every corner, often in places you would never think to look.

That reality comes crashing back when I pick James' clothes out of the hamper to wash.

I feel something in the pocket of his pants, and I smile when I pull out the old photo, the words *James, age 12*, scribbled on the back. But when I turn it over, a coldness sweeps through me.

A twelve-year-old James stands with two people who are obviously his parents, and it hits me why he seemed familiar at first.

His eyes. The same sapphire blue as his father's.

James is Clay Saggel's son.

"Oh my God." I'm trembling, unable to look away from the picture. The resemblance is so clear now.

He lied to me. Out of all the things he could have hidden - this is the worst. The gut-punch I didn't see coming.

I've been such a fool, blinded by love.

"He's one of them..." I shake my head, trying to process it.

And then fear smacks me straight in the chest. He went into town this morning. To Fox Hollow. What if he went there to tell them he found me? No doubt Clay already put a bounty on me. Has this all been a game?

Ice pricks my skin as a million thoughts rush through me. Distrust cuts into my heart like a knife, even though there's a part of me that wants to believe he has a reason for hiding this from me.

Run, my head screams. *Get Lily and run.*

And I do.

I gather up our things, and make a sling for Lily, wrapping her against my body, then stuff the last of the formula into my backpack. I know I don't have much time. James will be back soon. And with him, Clay's men.

Betrayal, anger, the need to survive...that's what makes my legs move, even though I'm numb inside. I'm not even sure where I'm going, I just run, through the dense trees, slipping on muddy rocks, branches cutting into my arms.

I run until the sky turns a dark purple and Lily's cries alert me that she's hungry. But I have no way to warm up the formula, no fresh water.

"Shit," I cry out, not knowing what to do.

In the distance I see headlights. A road. I stumble down the steep hill, yelping when I twist my ankle. Fighting through the pain, I limp toward the highway, waving my hands for the next car to stop.

A truck slows, its headlights blinding.

"Please," I cry out. "I need help. Can you take me—"

A deep rumbling laugh fills the night's sky when a giant of a man steps out, two more jumping from the cargo bed. If I thought I was scared before, it's terror that consumes me now.

"Time to come home, darlin'," Clay says, walking toward me, a smirk stretching his lips, those blue eyes cold and callous as his hands wrap around my throat. "You've been a very bad girl." He leans closer, his foul breath on my cheek. "And you know what we do to bad girls, don't you, sweetheart?"

CHAPTER NINE

James

"Where the hell did you go, Marcie?" Dread fills me as I get back into my truck and start the engine. When I got back to my cabin and saw the front door wide open, I knew something was wrong.

At first I'd thought someone had found her, but there was no sign of a struggle. And her bag was gone, including the remaining formula. She's left on her own.

It was when I saw the old photo on the table that I knew why.

"Fuck." I slam my fist on the steering wheel. I should have told her. But she shouldn't have run. The thought of her and Lily out in these woods, alone, fills me with a panic I've never known before.

Especially when the sun drops and the stars

appear above me. There are wolves on the mountain, mountain lions, and bears.

"Come on, Marcie, where are you?" I pull onto the main highway, driving slowly, knowing I'm looking for a needle in a haystack.

But then I see the taillights of a truck stopped up ahead. It's dark, but I see the silhouettes of three men, and a woman who struggles against them.

Marcie.

They have her in the truck and are speeding away by the time I reach them. Other than trying to force them off the road, all I can do is follow behind. I can't risk Marcie and Lily getting hurt.

But I know where they're going.

The clubhouse.

All these years I've avoided confrontation with my father. But I know how this has to end. I make a call. The one I should have made years ago.

Family is family, but blood is thicker than water. My father started this war, but I will end it. Today. If I'd done it earlier, Marcie would have never been branded by the man who shares my name. But then maybe I would never have met her, touched her - loved her.

So I do what has to be done to save her.

"Detective Pearson? This is James Saggel. I'm ready to talk. But I need your help."

I give the man the details of the club, how many men will most likely be inside, including the civilians.

But even with the police involved, I know Marcie is in danger, and it scares the shit out of me.

Detective Pearson's words ring in my ear. "Wait for us to arrive. Don't do anything stupid before we get there."

I stay back, following the truck from a distance, and turning my headlights off as I approach the clubhouse. My plan is to wait for the police to arrive, but when I see it's my father who gets out of the truck and pulls Marcie roughly out with him, that primal part of my brain overtakes all rational thought.

I need to save my girls.

No matter the cost.

CHAPTER TEN
Marcie

Clay's fingers bruise my arm as he shoves me inside the old rundown building that smells like cheap alcohol and cigarettes. I glance around, half expecting James to be here, but he's not. And I'm starting to think I was wrong about him.

I ran from the only man who ever tried to help me, and now I'm in more trouble than I can get out of. I see the glint of metal under Clay's shirt, and I know he won't hesitate to use the gun on me if I try to fight him.

"Sit," the man who murdered my sister says, shoving me down by my shoulder, forcing me into a chair. "And make that kid shut the fuck up, or I will."

I try to soothe Lily, but she won't stop wailing. "She's hungry," I say, as the room starts to clear.

People smart enough to know their leader is volatile and about to lose his shit - on me. "I need to make her a bottle."

"Get the kid out of here." Clay snaps his fingers, and Mickey, one of the girls who'd helped me escape, scuttles across the room, giving me a look of pity before reaching for Lily.

I want to fight her, but I know my niece will be safer with her than here with me, considering what I can only imagine Clay has planned. A shiver races down my spine, but I need to stay strong - for Lily.

"Take care of her," I whisper, tears in my eyes before handing her to the woman.

Mickey nods, gathering Lily to her chest then rushing out of the room.

"Everyone else, out," Clay roars, and the last of the men disappear, leaving us alone.

He moves toward me, each step calculated and slow, meant to scare me. But it's the flash of excitement in his eyes, at what he's about to do to me that truly terrifies me. And I realize how wrong I was thinking James and him look anything alike.

They share the same sapphire blue eyes, but that's where the similarities stop.

James might be a giant of a man, but there's no brutality in him. Not like his father.

"You think you can run from me, darlin'?" He

grips my jaw roughly. "You belong to me. I marked you as my own."

I twist my face out of his hands. "You can do what you want to me, but I'll never be owned by anyone."

He laughs, hard and cruel. "I was going to make a few pennies on that virgin cunt of yours, but I think I'll take it for my own."

I slap him, hard. It's a knee-jerk reaction, one that I regret instantly. Because the next thing I know I'm being flung across the room.

Pain shoots through my shoulder and cheek when I hit something hard. And then he's on top of me - until he's not.

"I'll kill you for this," a man roars, sounding more like wild animal than human. It's a roar filled with vengeance.

My head is dizzy, and I have to blink a few times to see the hulk of a man standing over Clay, one hand fisted in the collar of his shirt, the other pulled back to strike the man I now know is his father.

James gets a few blows in before Clay is able to shake him off.

"James," I cry out when I see Clay reach for his gun.

But it's too late, the weapon is already drawn, and pointed straight at James' chest.

"You little bastard," Clay spits out.

James glances over at me, clearly more concerned for my own safety than his own. And I feel like a fool for ever thinking he'd betray me.

"It's over," James says, looking back at his father. "You can put a bullet in me, but you're not walking out of here, not without handcuffs or in a casket."

"What did you do?" Clay releases the safety on the gun, cocking it.

"What I should have done years ago."

"You called the fucking pigs on me? You know if I go down, you go down with me."

"Maybe," James spits out, giving me a sideways glance. "But it'll be worth it."

Clay looks at me then, his eyes narrowing. "You turned me in for a piece of ass?" He points the gun at me, then. "Is that what you're telling me, son?"

I see the fear in James' face. "I turned you in to protect the people who can't protect themselves from you."

"You think I'm a monster because I take what I want? Because I do what I have to in order to survive?"

"You are a monster," I say, standing. "You killed my sister—"

"I loved your sister," Clay yells, face red with rage. "She died giving birth."

"Because you wouldn't let her go to a hospital." I don't care that the gun is still pointed at me, I'm fueled by anger, by rage.

"Just like you killed Mother," James says, moving so that he's standing between me and his father. "You abandoned her when she needed you most. I won't let you hurt anyone else." It's then that James lunges at him, and the gun goes flying.

The two men fight, fists swinging, blood spraying from their noses and mouths.

And then the door flies open and a swarm of police enter, yelling orders. James puts his hands up, and I sink to my knees, knowing it's over.

But Clay doesn't give up that easy. He reaches for the gun and points it at me. A blast rings out through the room and I gasp, waiting for the bullet to pierce me. But no pain comes, because James jumps in front of me, taking the shot himself.

More shots are fired, and Clay drops the gun, eyes wide as he looks down at the three bright red wounds on his chest, before collapsing to the ground, dead.

But it's James who I focus on. Blood pools under his palms where he holds his stomach.

"Oh God," I cry out, placing my own hands over the wound. "Someone help."

More sirens wail and officers are yelling at me to move away from him, but I refuse.

"You're going to be okay," James says, reaching up to brush his knuckles across my cheek. "I'm..." He winces, his face pale. "I'm so sorry...I...I love you..." His eyes close and his hand drops to his side.

"James," I cry out. "No, no, no. Someone, please, help him. He can't die. Please."

But I'm being pulled away, kicking and screaming, large hands restraining me as a team works on him.

"You have to come with me, ma'am," an officer says calmly, like my whole world isn't crashing down around me.

Because that's what James is - my world.

I didn't know what living was until I met him. Had no idea what love meant. But now, watching my man bleed out on the dirty floor of the hell I escaped from, I know what it means now - sacrifice.

And James may have just paid the ultimate sacrifice for me.

As the police officer leads me away, I know I

need to make sure that his sacrifice is for something.

————

After hours being interrogated by police and social workers and checked over by doctors and nurses, I'm completely exhausted and a mess. Because I still know nothing about James' condition. All anyone has told me is that he's in surgery.

Mickey stays with me in the waiting room, helping me with Lily when she's finally returned to my care.

"You really love him, don't you?" Mickey asks, taking my hand.

"Yeah, I do," I tell her, chewing on my bottom lip and glancing up at the damn clock that doesn't seem to be moving.

"I'm glad. You both deserve some happiness."

"You know James?" I glance over at her.

"I was friends with his mom." Mickey sighs. "She was a good woman. She kept Clay in line. For a time anyway. He wasn't always such an evil man. But after she died, he lost his mind...and then James left..."

"What was James like before?" I ask, not sure I want to know, but also needing to.

"He was a good boy." A small smile tugs at her lips. "More like his mama, than..."

"Clay," I offer.

She nods. "Sure, he got into some trouble. But the boy always had a sensitive heart. I wasn't surprised when he ran off. Clay told everyone that he died, but I knew the truth. Even as a kid, he'd spend hours up on that mountain, exploring the woods. After his mom died, he'd disappeared for days. I always thought his heart belonged there." She squeezes my hand. "It seems right that it's where he found you."

"Oh God, what am I going to do if he doesn't—"

"You can't think like that. James is a survivor, just like you. He'll make it."

But as she says the words a man in a white coat with a grim look on his face approaches. "Are you Marcie?" he asks.

I nod, a lump forming in my throat, my belly constricting with fear. "Is...is he all right?"

"You need to come with me."

CHAPTER ELEVEN

James

When I wake up, my first thought is on my girls.

My girls.

The ones I betrayed. The ones I hurt. Fuck.

But I'm alive. And I will do what it takes to set things straight. I move, wanting to get out of this fucking hospital bed. I rip the IV from my arm, my only thought on finding Marcie and Lily. I will spend every day of my life fixing what I've wronged.

"Hold up, there," a doctor says, coming into my room. "You aren't going anywhere."

"I have to," I say. "I need my Marcie—"

He cuts me off. "You just came out of surgery, you nearly died. You are staying in this hospital bed even if it means restraining you."

I press my hand to my chest, the pain excruciating now that I've been brought back to reality.

"Fuck." I close my eyes, wanting, more than anything, for Marcie to be here. Wanting to wipe the pain from her eyes. When she looked at me back at the clubhouse, it was like she thought I was a stranger.

Maybe I am.

I lean back on the bed, pain ripping through my belly, but it's the pain in my chest that hurts more. God, I've lost her. I know it. But at least now she's safe. My father will never hurt her or anyone else again. She's free to live the life she wants. I dig my palms into my eyes and try not to panic. But I need to know that she's okay.

Fuck, I'd lost it when I saw my father on top of her, knowing his intentions. And then he'd fired the shot. I didn't think, just reacted, jumping in front of her. And I'd do it a million times over.

"I need to get out of here," I say, but when I open my eyes, the doctor is gone.

In his place is Marcie, holding Lily in her arms. The pain I've caused covering her face, her once bright eyes are dark. And it kills me to think that I did this to her.

"Marcie." I try to sit up, wincing when I manage it.

"Don't," she says, moving to my side. "You're going to open your stitches."

"I don't care. I just...I needed to know you're all right."

Her brows draw down. "No, James, I'm not all right."

"Fuck. You have no idea how sorry I am. I wanted to tell you. I was going to tell you—"

"I know." She rocks Lily in her arms, worry still tugging at her mouth. "I'm not all right, James, because for a moment I thought...I thought you died. And it..." A small sob escapes her lips and tears fill those beautiful hazel eyes of hers. "It was the worst thing I've ever felt."

I want to wrap her in my arms, and I reach for her, ignoring the pain that shoots through my gut. "Come here."

"I don't want to hurt you."

"The only thing hurting me is not being close to you." I pull her into my arms, Lily sleeping soundly between us.

"I was so scared."

I kiss the top of her head. "I felt the same way when I came back to the cabin and found you gone."

"I shouldn't have left—"

"We can go over all our shouldn'ts, but it doesn't change anything...and you're here now. Safe."

She glances up at me. "You saved me, again."

"I'd save you a million times over, take a thousand bullets, fight through any rainstorm to make sure you're safe. You're my heart, Marcie. You're what it beats for."

She places her hand on my chest. "You're mine too."

"I love you." I smile down at Lily who squirms between us. "Both of you. And I know that's fast to say. That you probably need time to figure out what you want—"

"I know what I want." She strokes a hand over my cheek and beard.

"Yeah?" I swallow, praying to God that it's me. "What's that?"

"I want the heart of this mountain man."

"You have it."

She grins. "And you have mine. I love you, James."

I let out the breath I didn't realize I'd been holding in and kiss her. "Fuck, I hope this is real and not heaven."

She chuckles. "It's real. But you did just get shot. You need to rest."

"Not before I ask you something..." Nerves make my stomach flutter, and I take her hand and bring it to my lips. "Will you marry me, Marcie. Be my wife?"

Her eyes widen.

I continue, my words tumbling from my lips. "We can move to the city. I can buy a house with a yard, and—"

"No."

"No?" My gut sinks.

Her eyes twinkle. "No, I don't want to move to the city. I love the cabin. The mountain. It's a perfect place to raise Lily, and maybe one or two of our own in the future. We might have to add a couple more rooms, but I think—"

"So, that's a yes?"

A huge smile brightens her whole face. "Yes. I want to marry you, James. You have my heart, always and forever."

EPILOGUE I

James

One year later....

"What do you think?" I ask, holding my beautiful wife in my arms and looking at the renovations that are finally done - and just in time. Because it won't be long before our new additions will be here.

"It's perfect." Marcie twists in my arms, her large belly between us, and smiles up at me. "Now we'll finally get some privacy."

I chuckle, kissing her, then glance over at where Lily and Banjo are playing in the dirt. Lily squeals in delight when Banjo licks her face.

"Speaking of privacy," I say, picking Lily up and tossing her in the air, making her giggle. "It's time for you to have a nap."

"No, no, no," she says in her baby voice. "P*aaaay. Pease.*"

"You can play after your nap. Plus, you get to sleep in your new room."

She claps her hands in delight as I take her into the cabin, cleaning her up before laying her down in her crib.

With the twins on the way, soon this mountain is going to get a whole lot busier, and noisier.

I shut the door and find Marcie in our new master bedroom. She's stretched out on the king-sized bed, and she groans in delight when she sees me. "Oh my God, this bed is so comfortable. I don't think I've ever felt anything better."

I chuckle, leaning over her and pressing my mouth to hers, then raise a brow. "Nothing?"

She laughs, fingers playing with the buttons on my shirt. "You know what I meant."

"I think you're going to have to convince me that I'm not going to be replaced by a memory foam mattress."

Her fingers are already peeling away my shirt, then moving down to my jeans. "Or maybe you need to remind me why I love you more," she teases.

"I thought I did that last night." I nip at her bottom lip, sliding my hands under her shirt and finding her nipple. She whimpers when I flick it, then lower my mouth for a taste.

"Mmmm," she moans. "I think I need a repeat."

I don't hesitate. I undress us both and lose myself in her. Each touch, each kiss like it's the first and last. She runs her hand over my length, her eyes lit with want. My only goal is to make her this happy forever.

She rolls on top of me, straddling me, easing down on my cock, my hands running over her swollen belly. God, she looks like an angel.

"What?" she asks, her hips swiveling as I fill her up the way she needs. Her auburn hair falling in her eyes. I brush it back, drawing her closer for a kiss. Her lips are soft, her skin is like butter, and my cock grows as I take her, as I make her mine all over again.

"God, I fucking love you."

She smiles, her tits bouncing as she reaches the edge of her pleasure, and I hold on to her, loving the way it feels when she reaches euphoria. When we come together, our bodies ignite as one. I know I'm the luckiest guy in the world.

I always thought that I'd live my life alone in these mountains. Never thought I'd get a second chance. But with Marcie every day, my heart beats more wild, more alive.

EPILOGUE II

Marcie

Five years later ...

Lily is shrieking with delight as she steps in the river bed, the cool water covering her feet, splashing around her ankles, her curly auburn hair bouncing as she moves. Banjo weaves through the water before running in the lush forest, the happiest dog I've ever known. Lily reaches out her little girl hand, needing her daddy to hold on tight to help with balance. James is there, offering Lily his hand - just like he always is. There for his family.

The heart of this mountain.

"I got you, little sparrow," James tells Lily, my heart melting as I watch them together.

I kneel on the blanket spread over the pebbled shore of the river, reaching into my picnic basket and taking out the chocolate cake I baked last night. In an instant, our four-year-old twins, Benson and Bradley, are asking for a slice.

"Be patient, it's Lily's birthday, let's wait for her."

Baby Abby coos in her little basket, and she kicks her feet up, reaching for her toes. Six months old and a blessing to be sure. When I found out I was expecting again, I remember running to James' woodshop, tears in my eyes. He knew it before I said a word.

"Guess I'll be pulling out the cradle again, won't I?"

Of course we aren't in the same cabin, we outgrew that by the time our Lily was one. Our new home is on the same piece of land, there was no way we were leaving this mountain. I may be used to challenges in life, but a toddler and a woodfire stove stressed me out! James and a crew from Idaho built our home. The crew leader, Jax, told us if we ever want to relocate, there was a place called Miracle Mountain that would welcome us with open arms.

It was a sweet offer, but there is no way I am leaving the mountains of Fox Hollow. Being here is being home. James is the heart of this mountain and it's where I want to raise our family.

"Mama!" Lily giggles. "Daddy is soaking wet!"

I look up and see James' pants are wet all the way through. I smile, meeting my husband's eyes. He looks even more handsome than he did five years ago, when he saved my life.

When he sacrificed himself for me.

It still brings tears to my eyes, remembering the day at the clubhouse, when James took the bullet and almost lost his life.

I wipe the tears from my eyes, this is a day to celebrate. To celebrate Lily's life. She may be technically my niece and James' half-sister, but in every way that matters, she is our daughter, and she lost so much the day she entered the world. I carry my sister's memory in my heart, doing all that I can to impart her memory on the child she will never see grow.

"Why you sad, Mama?" Bradley asks.

"They are happy tears," I tell my little guy. "I'm just so happy to be here."

"Me too," Lily says, coming over to us and reaching for a towel to dry her feet. "I love the water. And the forest. And the whole wide world!"

James and I laugh, she is a ball of energy, spirited and so full of life. "You know the forest is where I first met you and your mama," James says, reaching for candles in the basket and placing them on Lily's cake. "It's a special place for all of us."

"I'm gonna get married on a mountain one day," Lily says with a long sigh, suddenly seeming so much older than five.

"There's no rush to grow up, Sparrow," I tell her.

"But I want to be big. I want to be a mama and have a bunch of babies and live happily ever after."

James chuckles, tousling Lily's red hair. "There is time for that, but today, let's eat cake."

"Make a wish first," Benson says.

I light the five candles, grateful for the perfect summer day. As a family, we opt for small, private celebrations. Being together is the only party we need.

We sing happy birthday to our little girl, and I wonder what it will be like, one day, to see her all grown. As she closes her eyes to make a wish, I do too. I wish that Lily can always be this happy, this full of love and light. That her heart will always know where home is.

She blows them out and when she opens her eyes, she gasps, looking up in the sky. A rainbow appears, painting the sky with pastels and I feel our hearts collectively swoon. The sun always shines after the storm.

ALSO BY FRANKIE & C.M.

Hammers and Veils

Stripped Bare

Nailed Down

Scr*wed Tight

Drilled Deep

Love Without Limits

Naughty Scot

Dirty Brit

Unruly Norse

Filthy Irish

Booty Call Series

Bootyogomy

Bootyversary

Humpany

Booty Camp

Get Some Series

A.D..I.D.A.S. (All Day I Dream About Sex)

G.O.A.T. (Greatest of All Time)

T.Y.P.O. (Take Your Pants Off)

Standalones

Heart of the Mountain

Game Day Baby

FRANKIE LOVE

Frankie Love writes filthy-sweet stories about bad boys and mountain men.

As a thirty-something mom to six who is ridiculously in love with her own bearded hottie, she believes in love-at-first-sight and happily-ever-afters.

She also believes in the power of a quickie.

Find Frankie here:
www.frankielove.net

C.M. SEABROOK

C.M. Seabrook writes hot, steamy romances with possessive bad boys, and the passionate, fiery women who love them. Swoonworthy romances from the heart!

Find C.M. here:
www.cmseabrook.com

For something a little different, read **Chantel Seabrook's** Shifter, Reverse Harem, and Fantasy books here https://amzn.to/2MTiItI

NAUGHTY SCOT PREVIEW

"I'm comin'," I grumble, tossing on a shirt and a pair of breeks when the knocking on my cabin door continues.

I open the front door, sure it's Gregor here to ask which field I want the sheep to graze this morn'. But it's not the lad I'm expecting. An older woman, carrying a bundle in her arms that I'm supposin' is a bairn, peers at me over wired rimmed glasses.

"Can I help you?" I ask, running a hand over my beard.

We don't get many visitors in these parts. Other than the men who work for me, the small town just east of here, and few smaller crofts that dot the hills surrounding my own, it's just grass, sheep, and hills for miles around.

"Are you Kier MacKinnon?" the woman asks, peering around me, trying to look into the cabin.

"Who's askin'?" A sense of foreboding sits heavy on my chest, and I get the impression the woman is scrutinizing me. I rake my fingers back through my hair trying to look more presentable, but it's not much use.

"I'm Martha O'Connelly, from the Social Services Coalition."

"Is this a charity thing? Are you raising money?"

Martha shakes her head, resting the babe on her shoulder, and patting it's back. "No, quite the opposite. Can I come in?"

Frowning, I consider the question. An old biddy asking to come into my cottage with a wee one is the last thing I was expecting. But I'm not going to deny this woman what she wants.

"Did you have some car trouble, or get lost?" I ask, prying her for information as I lead her into the small living area. "It's easy to lose your way in the highlands—"

"No. There's a purpose to my visit."

I frown at her and nod, glancing back down at the bairn. If I weren't a hundred percent certain that the wee one wasn't mine, I'd probably be pacing the floor right now wondering about the news she's here to deliver.

"Tea?" I ask, attempting manners. It's been a long arse while since I've needed to use them.

"No, that's fine," she says, her gaze scrutinizing every detail of the house. "This is your home, then?"

"After my parents passed, I never moved into the main house, just kept back here. Fine for a bloke like me."

"Right, well, the thing is Kier, I have some rather untimely news." She frowns, her lips forming a thin line. "You may want to sit for it."

"Just tell me, what's this all about?"

"I gather you never received my messages?"

"Gregor is my errand boy, but he rarely remembers to fetch the mail. Was it important?"

"Quite. It's about your sister, Mollie."

There's that unsettling feeling again, but now it's in the pit of my stomach. "Haven't seen her for two years. She left home the day she turned eighteen and never came back. Have you seen her then?"

Martha sighs, taking a seat on the worn couch, bairn still in her arms. "That's why I'm here, Kier. She's gone."

"What do you mean, gone? She hasn't been around in ages." I try to keep the bitterness from my voice, but it just about broke my parents' hearts when she left without a backward glance. Didn't even have the decency to come home for her own parents' funeral.

Martha pats the seat cushion beside her. "Why don't you have a seat."

I do as she asks. "What is it then?"

"Your sister has died, Kier, and this wee one is her son."

————

Four weeks later...

I'd do it all over again, in a heartbeat. Aye, of course I would. The bairn is my family, and so of course I'll do what I must to keep him close.

But I never expected to be twenty-four-years-old with a wee one to look after. Before this, I never looked after a soul besides myself. I keep a low profile, my head down. I do the work of ten men on my farm and I go to bed exhausted every night. I don't have time to worry about women, about lassies looking for a fun time.

It's never been my style. But now I am going to have a woman living in my house.

"You want the bed here, in this corner?" Gregor

asks from the spare bedroom across the hall from the nursery.

The social worker had insisted I couldn't keep a baby in a cottage without running water, so I'd moved back into the main house where Mollie and I grew up. It's so much bigger than the cottage, but the place feels...wrong. Sheets still cover furniture, rooms are bare after I'd had to sell most anything of value last fall to pay off my father's incurred debt. A debt he'd managed to keep hidden until I'd taken over the books after he passed.

I've managed to get the accounts in order, even hired a couple more men to tend to the sheep, but I should be out on the moor, not here consoling a crying bairn.

As if on cue, Brodie starts wailing - his favorite thing to do, morning, noon, and night.

"When does the nanny arrive?" Gregor asks, wiping his hands on his kilt once he's finished setting up the bed. For a young bloke, he's a hard worker. And getting the main house put in working order is a task I need help with, especially since I have a newborn strapped to my chest in a sling.

"Hopefully soon," I tell him, placing Brodie on my shoulder and rocking him.

"I think he's hungry," Gregor says.

"You want to take care of him?"

Gregor puts his hands up and chuckles. "No. I'm not good with wee ones."

I grunt and leave Gregor to continue straightening the room and go to the kitchen to fetch Brodie a bottle.

The house is full of ghosts, broken promises, and memories, and I miss the small, simple confines of my cottage. But the main house has heat, and I realize that this wee boy needs that consistently. I may be a mountain of a man, but I'm not completely daft.

"It's okay, little one," I say, patting his back and placing the bottle to his mouth. He latches on straight away and the moment the squawking stops my shoulders fall.

I've been a ball of tension since Brodie came into my life. After Martha broke the news to me, about my sister, I was a mess. The idea of her gone, forever, shook me up. She was so young, and while the girl always had a knack for getting into trouble, she was family. And I'd never wished her anything but goodwill. But complications in childbirth means she's now watching over her boy from above, not cradling him in her arms.

So, I did what needed to be done and got this house in order for little Brodie. I fetched a crib, nappies, and bottles, but I'm in utterly over my head. One of the first things I did was call Tansy. She was my mum's best friend, though she's now moved to America. She told me I needed a nanny, straightaway. I took down the number of a service she'd heard about and made the call, but now, nearly four weeks have passed and I'm still waiting.

I was told the nanny would be here two days ago, but there hasn't been any sighting of her. Maybe the girl changed her mind. I'll have to make another call to the agency if she doesn't show up by tomorrow.

The bottle is finished, which means Brodie is back to fussing. Probably needs a nappy change, a burp. I never knew how much care a wee one needs.

I can see the sheep through the window, needing to be put in the lower field. I haven't checked on my farm in weeks and I know the crew are wondering where I've gotten off to.

There's a knock on the door, and I say a silent prayer that it's the woman I've been waiting on.

A screaming bairn in my arms, I walk toward the front of the main house and wince when I catch my reflection in the full-length mirror. Brodie spit up over my shirt earlier and I'd taken it off, so I'm currently bare-chested. But at least I'm wearing breeks.

I think about running upstairs and putting on a shirt, but the knocking grows more insistent.

When I open the front door, it takes me a moment to realize that it's a woman who stands there, because she's covered head to toe in mud and dirt, and god only knows what else considering the smell. Tangles of wild brown curls are plastered against her face, and big hazel eyes blink up at me, widening when she takes in my appearance.

But despite her obvious attempt to hold back tears, she stretches out a hand, and says, "I'm Elsie Stewart. Your new nanny."

Printed in Great Britain
by Amazon

24099993R00057